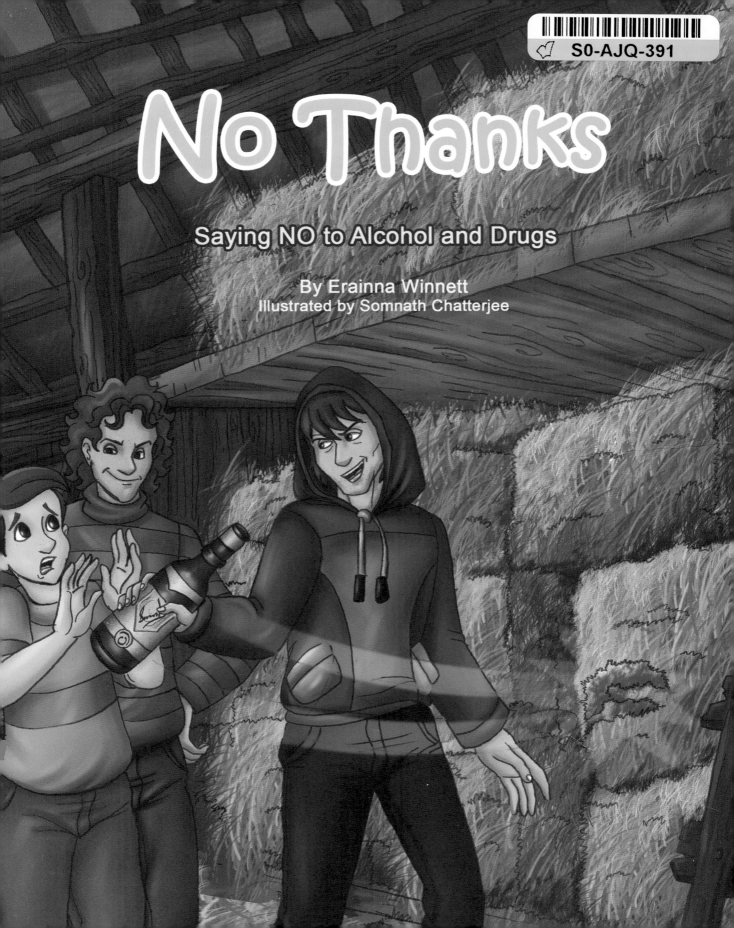

No Thanks

Saying NO to Alcohol and Drugs

By Erainna Winnett

Illustrated by Somnath Chatterjee

No Thanks!
Saying NO to Alcohol and Drugs
Text copyright © 2013 by Erainna Winnett
Illustrations copyright © 2013 by Somnath Chatterjee

Author: Erainna Winnett
Illustrator: Somnath Chatterjee

Printed in the United States of America

Summary: Blake and Colton face a tough decision when Colton's older brother and his persuasive friend offer them alcohol and drugs.

ISBN:061590775X
ISBN: 978-0615907758

Library of Congress Cataloging-in-Publication Data
Winnett, Erainna
No Thanks!
Saying NO to Alcohol and Drugs
Library of Congress Control Number:2013919602

www.counselingwithheart.com

To my dad for always being there for me. I love you!

As the school bus rumbled uphill, Blake hefted his backpack. The driver would yell if he stood up now. But he wanted to get off already, race toward home, and start practicing his kicks and hand chops.

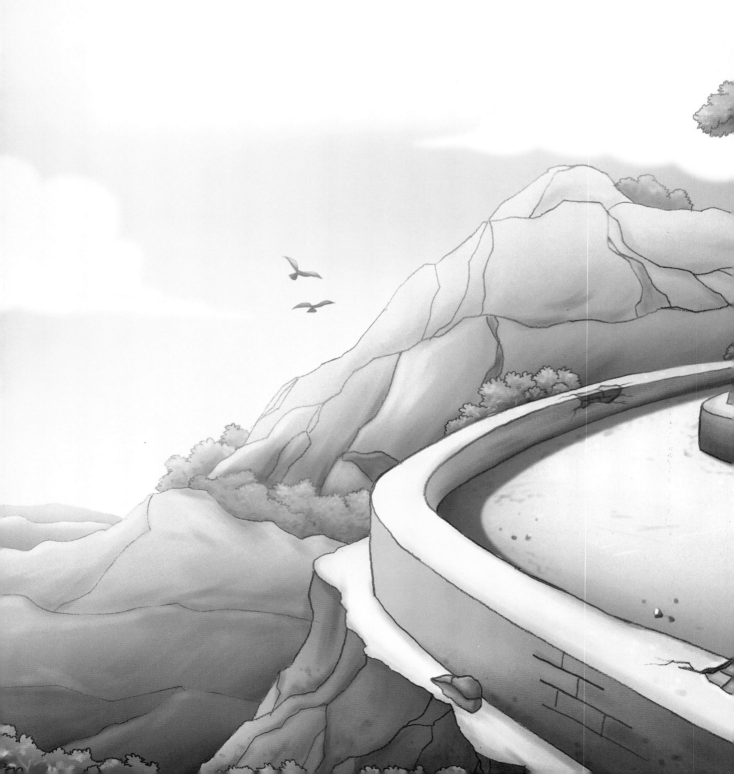

His best friend, Colton, elbowed him. "You and Jacob practicing karate?" Colton asked.

"Yeah." Blake nodded. "Only two more days until the tournament! Dad says if I do well, he'll buy me that tablet we saw on the internet!"

"That's cool," Colton said.

Tension and excitement twisted in Blake's stomach. He could almost feel the tablet's screen beneath his fingertips. With coaching help from Colton's older brother, Jacob, Blake was confident he'd shine at the tournament.

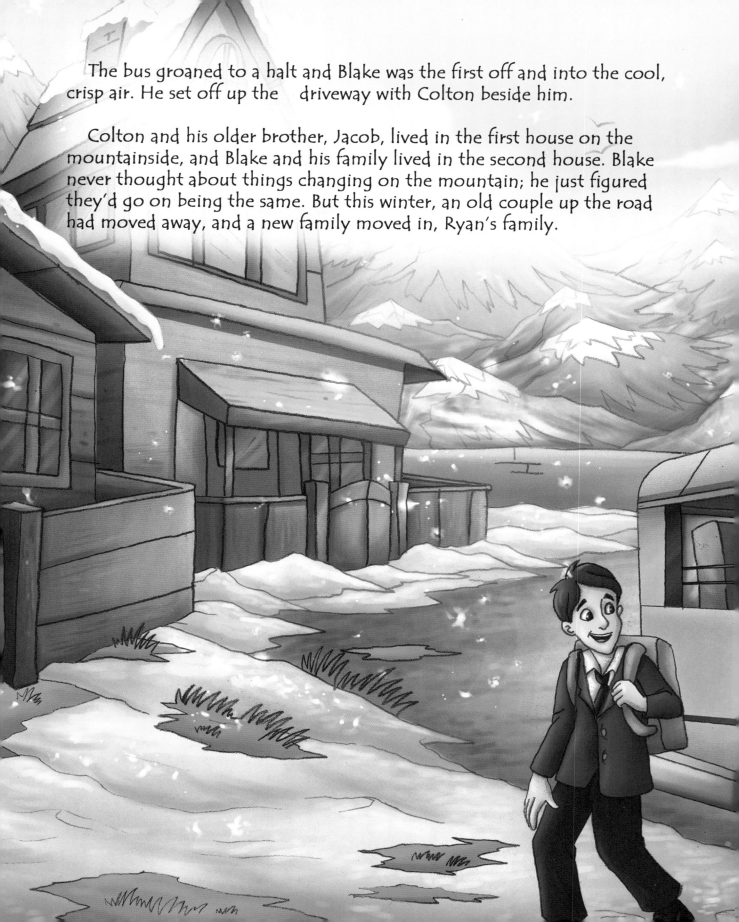

The bus groaned to a halt and Blake was the first off and into the cool, crisp air. He set off up the   driveway with Colton beside him.

Colton and his older brother, Jacob, lived in the first house on the mountainside, and Blake and his family lived in the second house. Blake never thought about things changing on the mountain; he just figured they'd go on being the same. But this winter, an old couple up the road had moved away, and a new family moved in, Ryan's family.

Ryan always had a quick answer. He could talk his way into or out of anything. Even the high school teachers had a hard time disagreeing with him. But Ryan had changed things on the mountain. Since Ryan came around, Jacob had changed. He didn't want to hang out with Blake and Colton any more. He said they were lame and immature. Instead, he and Ryan hung out over the ridge, by the empty barn in the Pierces' field.

"Hey, guys," Blake called as Jacob and Ryan sauntered past.

Ryan was so lanky in his dark hoodie and tight jeans that he reminded Blake of a wintertime tree.

"Um, Jacob, can we practice my kicks as soon as we're home?" Blake asked.

Jacob shrugged. "Might be busy," he mumbled.

Blake felt a jolt of disappointment. "Busy doing what?" he asked. "Look, man, I need more help before the tournament. I've only got two days. You promised you'd coach me."

"Yeah, whatever," Jacob muttered .

"Jacob's got other things on his mind." Ryan smirked. "Jacob's my main man."

Blake didn't know what Ryan was talking about. "I really need help," he repeated.

"How about coming to the old barn?" Ryan asked. "Then maybe Jacob can help you later with your Samurai stuff."

Blake bit his lip. "Sure, I guess," he finally mumbled.

"Hey, Colton, you want to play with the big boys too? "Ryan called. Colton shrugged but fell into step.

Blake and Colton followed the older kids up the mountain, past the houses, and across the field to the barn. Blake leaned in the doorway, staring at the bales of musty hay. He couldn't see what the attraction was. He'd rather be at home in the basement, learning how to make the sides of his hands into lethal weapons. Not that he was allowed to use them unless he was in karate class or a tournament. Still, it was a cool skill to master.

Ryan crossed the barn and slid a hand into the hay. He pulled out a bottle with water in it. Uncapping the lid, he took a swig and then held the bottle out to Blake. "Have some," he said. "You can sweat it out later when you do your Samurai kicks."

"What is it?" Blake asked.

Ryan grinned. "Pure spring water," he said. Something about the glint in his eyes made Blake suspicious.

"Seriously, what is it?" he asked.

"It's vodka," Jacob said, sounding nervous. "Ryan swiped it from home."

"Cool place to stash it," Ryan said. "Have some."

Blake took a step back and shook his head. His stomach churned with anxiety. "No thanks."

"It's no big deal," Ryan said. "Jacob drinks it."

"I said, no thanks," Blake repeated.

Ryan shrugged and handed the bottle to Jacob." Maybe you'll like my other secret better."

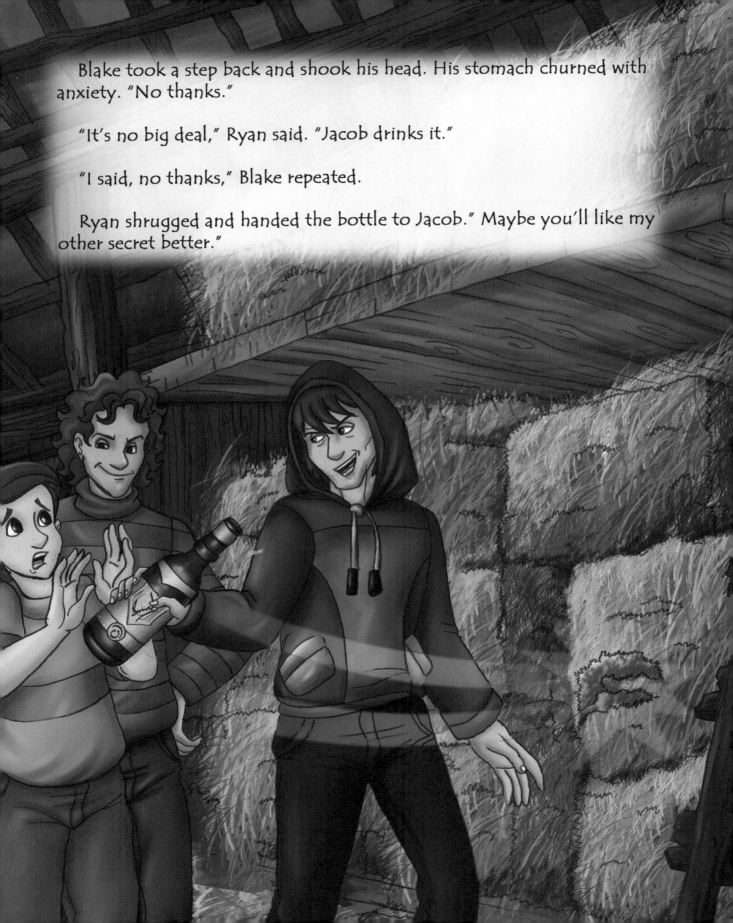

He stuck his skinny arm into the hay again and pulled out a plastic bag that he passed to Jacob with a wink.

Blake stared at the bag. Inside it were greeny-brown, dried leaves, some rolled into small cigarettes.

"What's that?" he asked.

Colton knew. "It's pot! What are you doing with this stuff?" he asked his brother.

Jacob shrugged, his eyes sliding away. "We come over here and smoke sometimes," he explained. "It's no big deal. You want to try it?"

"Mom and Dad will kill us if they find out!" Colton said.

Jacob laughed uneasily. "Chill out. We're not hurting anyone."

"Blake, you seriously need to try some," Ryan said, holding the bag out for Blake.

Blake's mind raced and whirled. He couldn't believe this was happening, on a normal afternoon, in this place where he and Jacob and Colton had built swings and flown kites.

"I gotta run now," Blake announced. "I gotta go practice."

"Yeah, but try this first," Ryan said. "It will relax you."

Suddenly, the words of Blake's instructor filled his head and spilled out of his mouth. "At karate class we learn to keep a clear mind. And to do kicks, I need to be coordinated and focused – not relaxed and stoned."

"Kid's not getting the message," Ryan said, rolling his eyes. He took the vodka from Jacob and shoved it into the hay.

Blake hopped anxiously from one foot to the other. He felt like a boa constrictor was wrapped around his chest. He could hardly breathe against the pressure.

"Come on," Ryan persisted. "It'll be fun." He opened the bag and took out a marijuana joint. Blake backed away , almost stumbling against Colton.

Ryan pulled a lighter from one pocket. The flame shone bright.

Colton might smoke it, Blake thought. Colton might smoke it because Jacob is his brother. Then if I don't smoke, Colton might not be my buddy anymore. I might lose my best friend. He'll take sides with his brother, not with me.

A stab of fear made Blake's knees weak. He couldn't imagine life on the mountain without Colton being part of it.

Then he remembered one more thing his karate instructor had told the class: if you have to face a crisis, do it with courage.

Blake stopped shifting from foot to foot. He used his firmest voice. "I'm not into this," he said, then turned and walked away.

Patches of melting snow crunched as Blake left the barn and crossed the field. It seemed to stretch on forever. He'd never felt so lonely. His legs had never felt so heavy. He listened for footsteps behind him, but all he heard was laughter.

Then he heard someone running. "Hey, buddy, wait up!" Colton called.

Blake swung around. "Did you smoke it?" he asked.

"Nah," Colton said. "I told Ryan I had asthma when I was a kid, and I hate the smell of smoke."

A grin stretched Blake's face. "Race you!" he shouted. "I gotta go practice my chops and kicks!"

Saying "NO" To Alcohol and Drugs

Even when you want to say NO to alcohol and drugs, you might not know how. Here are ten ways you can say NO.

1. Keep repeating yourself, even if you feel like a broken record: "No thanks, no thanks, no thanks." When you keep saying the same thing, the other person will give up asking you.

2. Be too cool. You can say: "No way man, that's not my thing."

3. Change the subject. You can say: "Hey, man, what'd you think about the game last night?"

4. State an appointment. You can say: "My parents are waiting for me at home."

5. Use humour. You can say: "No way, I heard that stuff turns your tongue blue!" Be a goof!

6. Suggest something different to do.

You can say: "Nah, let's go grab something to eat instead."

7. Give the cold shoulder. This means that you ignore the person, move away from them and keep walking.

8. Use avoidance. If you know someone is using drugs or alcohol, avoid their company.

9. State the facts. You might say: "The smell of smoke gives me a headache" or "I don't like being out of control."

10. Use your parents. For example: "My parents would kill me if they found out."